Sports Day

For Christine, my wonderful
Ricky Rocket editor

Find out more about **Ricky Rocket** at
www.shoo-rayner.co.uk

First published in 2006 by Orchard Books
First paperback publication in 2007

ORCHARD BOOKS
338 Euston Road, London NW1 3BH
Orchard Books Australia
Hachette Children's Books
Level 17/207 Kent St, Sydney, NSW 2000

ISBN-10: 1 84616 041 3 (hardback)
ISBN-13: 978 1 84616 041 7 (hardback)

ISBN-10: 1 84616 397 8 (paperback)
ISBN-13: 978 1 84616 397 5 (paperback)

Text and illustrations © Shoo Rayner 2006

1 3 5 7 9 10 8 6 4 2 (hardback)
1 3 5 7 9 10 8 6 4 2 (paperback)

Printed in Great Britain

Orchard Books is a division of Hachette Children's Books.

Sports Day

Shoo Rayner

ORCHARD BOOKS

"**And on line one,** we have Ricky Rocket! Not many Earthlings on this planet, eh, Ricky?"

"Yes – I mean, no!" Ricky
stammered. Ricky was the only Earth
boy on the planet of Hammerhead.

"It's great to have you on the SatBrat Show, Ricky," the teevee presenter said. "Are you ready for our Big Quiz question?"

Ricky's heart thumped like the tail of an Andovian Kandaboo.

"Who is the current Galactic Dodecathlon champion?"

Ricky didn't hesitate.
"Spike Trackaway!"

"...is the right answer!"

Mum and Dad cheered along with the teevee audience. Even Ricky's annoying little sister Sue was excited.

"Ricky, you've won this week's star
prize: a Spike Trackaway T-shirt,
running cap, autographed book
and poster and – surprise – a
Spike Trackaway training day
at YOUR SCHOOL!"

Ricky was
stunned. Spike
Trackaway was
the greatest athlete
in the galaxy!

"Maybe Spike can turn you into a champion, Ricky," the presenter said. "Now, on with the show…"

"This is the best day of my life!" Ricky whooped.

THE SATBRAT SHOW

The Satbrat Show runs from 8.47 to 12.33 every Saturday morning.

The show is hosted by Bob Bubbaloola and sponsored by the Fizzywizzy Corporation.

The studio audience are often covered in green gunk when they arrive. Anyone who can **lick themselves clean in 30 seconds** wins a year's supply of Super Nova℠* candy.

* See Vorg World

Spike Trackaway came to Ricky's school the week before Sports Day. Ricky was allowed on stage as the headteacher, Mister Blister, introduced Spike.

"Here he is – the current Galactic Dodecathlon champion – Spike Trackaway!"

The cheering nearly knocked Ricky over!

"There are TWELVE different events in the Dodecathlon," said Mister Blister, "so Spike is an expert at TWELVE different sports! He's sure to get the best from you all."

THE GALACTIC DODECATHLON

There are twelve exciting events in the Dodecathlon.

 1 100 metres running

2 Long jump

 3 High jump

4 Shot Put

 5 Hurdles

6 Long Distance Running

 7 Underwater backstroke

8 200 metres flying

 9 Stick Throwing

10 Hoppity-skip jump

 11 Pole Vault

12 Bootball

Spike was amazing. He didn't have to shout or blow whistles. Everyone did what he said, even those who didn't like sport.

They practised the hundred metres
first. Roosta belted down the track
in under a parsec. Ricky and his
best friend Bubbles were left
standing in the dust.

"Come on," Spike smiled. "It's not
just about winning. It's about doing
the best you can."

Spike showed Ricky and Bubbles
how to power off the starting line
to gain a second or two. "You can
do so much better when you know
how," he explained.

Grip was the best at throwing
the shot put. He picked it up as
if it was made of foam, and tossed
it way down to the end of the field.

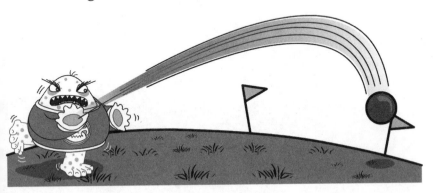

Ricky tried next. He lifted the
heavy ball onto his chest and
heaved it away from him.

"Just over two metres," said Spike.
"That's not bad." He showed Ricky
how to hold the ball up under his
chin. "Use your legs," he explained.
"Concentrate on where you want
it to land."

Ricky concentrated on a blade of
grass three metres away. He hurled
the shot again. It didn't hit the blade
of grass but it was close.

"Well done!" Spike smiled. "You can
do so much better when you know how."

"Great! It's long jump now," said
Bubbles. "I'm good at this."

Bubbles leapt off the jumping board.
A stream of blue bubbles poured out of
his trumpets as he sailed through the air.

"You can't beat jet propulsion!"
Spike laughed. Bubbles was easily
the best long jumper.

Ricky powered down the runway and leapt into the air. He was nowhere near as good as Bubbles.

Spike looked thoughtful. "You need to time your run-up better, Ricky." He showed Ricky how to count the paces before he jumped.

Ricky gained fifty centimetres on his best jump so far!

Ricky smiled at Spike. "OK, I get it. You can do so much better when you know how!"

GALACTIC
SPORTS STARS

Shayne Mooney
champion **bootballer**
has scored **2 million
goals** in his career

Goldy Carpright
galactic **underwater
long-distance** backstroke
champion

Downy Fluff
endurance floating
galactic record holder
**13 years, 14 days
and 12 minutes**

Frosty Snobug
speed skating
galactic record holder
723 kph over one
kilometre without atmosphere

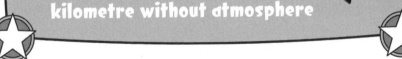

"**I'm exhausted!**" Ricky told Mum after school.

Bubbles had come back with him for tea. "You should've seen him, Mrs Rocket. Ricky was great!"

"But I'm not good at anything,"
Ricky complained. "I was
hoping Spike would teach
me how to *win* something."

"You *are* good!" Bubbles insisted,
"You worked really hard."

"But everyone else is so much better than me. Dooley's brilliant at the hurdles."

Bubbles laughed. "He should be, with all those legs."

"And Tammy Tweetle's brilliant at the high jump."

"She can float!"
Bubbles said.
"You did really
well when Spike
showed you how to
jump it sideways."

"What about the long-distance race, then?" Ricky was feeling sorry for himself.

"You came second in that! Only you and Shelby finished, and anyway, he's half-machine!"

Ricky sighed. "I'll just have to do my best on Sports Day."

Mum hugged Ricky. "You can't do more than your best!"

THE GALACTIC CHAMPIONSHIPS

This year, it is **Hammerhead's turn** to host this **sporting extravaganza.**

Sports stars come from all over the galaxy to compete in over 800 sporting disciplines, including:

Speed eating

Upside-down breath-holding

And the ever-popular **crawling marathon.**

All week long, Ricky practised what Spike had taught him. By Sports Day he felt much faster and stronger.

Mum and Dad cheered Ricky on and Sue screamed her support with the ear-splitting, blood-curdling, brain-jamming shrieks that little Earth girls are famous for all over the universe.

But however much he'd practised, it wasn't enough. Ricky was only an Earth boy.

While Ricky had to work hard to jump over every hurdle, Dooley slipped over them as if they were invisible.

"I wish I had six legs too," Ricky thought.

Tammy floated over the high jump

and Grip hurled the shot put across
the field.

Roosta tore down the
hundred-metre track

and Shelby slithered like
a well-oiled machine.

Bubbles won the long jump, trailing an impressive stream of bubbles.

At the end of the afternoon, Mister Blister made an announcement. "Congratulations, you all did splendidly! I've a surprise for you. Spike Trackaway, the Galactic Dodecathlon champion, has returned to present the winner's medals!"

Everyone was hoarse from cheering already, but they cheered even louder as Spike handed out the prizes.

Ricky clapped excitedly when Bubbles received his medal. "Well done, Bubbles! You deserve it!"

When all the medals had been
awarded, a silver shield still remained
on the medal table.

The applause died down and Spike
cleared his throat. "I know how hard it
is to be the best," He said. "Some
people win without trying, others have
to work hard for second place. That's
why I am a dodecathlete."

Spike explained how difficult it
was to be a good all-rounder.

"So," he continued, " I am pleased to award this shield to the school Hexathlon Champion. It goes to the competitor with the highest overall score in the SIX sports day events."

Mister Blister leapt onto the stage, waving a piece of paper.

"We've added up all the points,"
he said excitedly. "The school's
best all-round athlete and Hexathlon
Champion is...Ricky Rocket!"

Ricky didn't understand. He felt
hands and tentacules pushing him
towards the podium.

Spike shook his hand and gave him the shield. "Well done, Ricky! You worked hard for this."

Ricky couldn't believe his eyes.

"Thanks, Spike," he gulped.
"I couldn't have done it without you."

"You did it all by yourself,"
Spike smiled. "You only needed
to know how."

Ricky hugged the shield to his chest,
savouring the moment. Now this had
to be the best day in his life...ever!

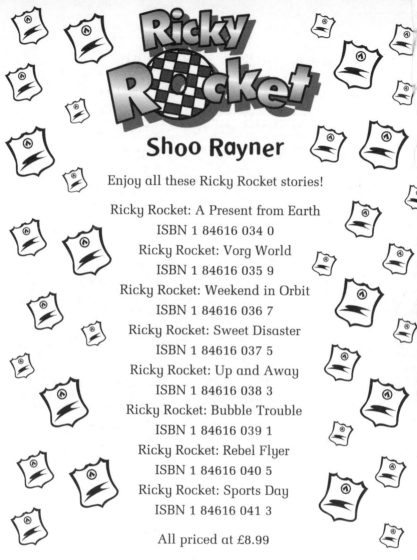

Ricky Rocket

Shoo Rayner

Enjoy all these Ricky Rocket stories!

All priced at £8.99

Orchard Crunchies are available from all good bookshops, or can be ordered
direct from the publisher: Orchard Books, PO BOX 29, Douglas IM99 1BQ
Credit card orders please telephone 01624 836000 or fax 01624 837033
or visit our internet site: www.wattspub.co.uk or e-mail: bookshop@enterprise.net for details.

To order please quote title, author and ISBN and your full name and address.
Cheques and postal orders should be made payable to 'Bookpost plc.'
Postage and packing is FREE within the UK
(overseas customers should add £1.00 per book).

Prices and availability are subject to change.